Chris Higgins

Illustrated by **Lee Wildish**

For Vinny, Zac, Ella and Jake.

And thank you, Ellen.

Chapter 1

I think someone's made a mistake. The year should begin in September, not January.

January's not much fun because:

🙁 Christmas is over and winter drags on and on and on.

🙁 You go to school in the dark, you come home in the dark.

☹ It's freezing cold and it rains all the time.

☹ Everyone gets colds and sore throats and snotty noses.

☹ You can't go out to play very much.

☹ And nothing will grow in our vegetable patch.

But in September:

☺ It's back to school! Yippee!

☺ The days are warm and sunny.

☺ After school you can still play out.

☺ Beans and spinach and pumpkins are growing in our vegetable patch.

2

🙂 Everybody is full of beans after our fab summer holiday.

🙂 And we have all shot up so much that Mum has to take us shopping for new school uniform.

We buy new shirts, new skirts and trousers, new sweatshirts, new socks, new PE kit, new underwear and a new winter coat if we've grown out of the old one.

We choose new pencil cases, new pencils, new pens, new rubbers, new rulers, new books to write in and a new bag if the old one is falling apart.

We also get fitted for new shoes and then we have our hair cut. All because we are going up a class in school.

'Oh dear,' says Mum, taking more money out of the cash machine. 'This is a very expensive time.'

It's a brand new start for everybody. Especially, this year, for my two brothers, Dontie and Stanley.

Dontie – who is eleven – is going to secondary school and Stanley is going to start at my school in reception class.

It's the first time Stanika will have been separated.

Stanika is Stanley and Anika. Stanley is going on five and Anika is going on three. They are always together, that's why we call them Stanika.

I'm worried they are going to miss each other.

I do rather a lot of worrying. Every day I make a Worry List. I find it helps. If I write down my worries, they don't happen. But if I don't write them down, they do.

This summer when I was on holiday in Cornwall I stopped keeping a Worry List. Then my brother Dontie fell off a cliff.

But that's another story.

My name is Mattie and I'm nine and a half. My sister V is seven and three-quarters. V is short for Vera Lynn but she doesn't like her name so we call her V.

Anika's going to stay at home with Mum, just the two of them, while everyone else goes to school, including my dad. He teaches art at the college. But sometime soon there will be three of them at home because my mum's having another baby.

Jellico will be there too, waiting for us to come home from school. Jellico is our scruffy, scrounging, scrumptious dog.

'Peace!' says Mum the night before school starts as she tucks us up in bed.

'School at last. Are you excited, Mattie?'

'Yesss!' I say, snuggling down and squeezing V round the middle which shows just how excited I am. My sister growls and throws my arm off but I don't care.

I can't wait to wear my new clothes.

I can't wait to use my new things which I've packed neatly in my new bag.

I can't wait to see my best friend, Lucinda.

'I'm not excited!' grumbles V. 'School is boring.'

My sister hates school. She's really clever with numbers and stuff but she can't read very well.

'You're not like your brother and sister,' said her last teacher, and the one before that, and the one before that. When teachers say this it makes V cross and when she gets cross, she gets into trouble.

'It'll be fine,' says Mum. 'New class, new teacher.'

'No it won't,' says V, very crossly indeed.

I'm with V on this. School won't be fine for her. It never is.

Mentally, I add her to my Worry List. Tonight it looks like this.

Worry List

1. How will Anika cope without Stan?

2. How will Stan cope without Anika?

3. How will V cope full stop?

Chapter 2

Lucinda has been to the Continent for her holidays with her dad who is an Accountant and her mum who is a Full-Time-Home-Maker.

'What's it like?' I ask.

'Big.'

Apparently the Continent is made up of lots of different countries which all speak different languages.

'What was the best bit?' I ask. She screws her face up to think for a long time then finally makes up her mind.

'Reading comics in the back of the car.'

Lucinda has brought me back presents from some of the places she visited. On the table in front of me are:

 a doll from Austria with a check apron and a hat with a ribbon

 a pair of castanets from Spain (castanets are little wooden things Spanish dancers click together and they make a noise)

 a tiny pair of clogs from Holland

 a donkey with straw baskets on its back from Portugal (not a real one)

 a pretty fan from Italy

a little lace handkerchief from Germany

I brought Lucinda back a present from Cornwall too. On the table in front of her is a small plaster figure of a Cornish piskie eating a pasty.

My part of the table looks a bit crowded. Lucinda's part of the table looks a bit empty.

'I love my piskie!' she says and my face breaks into a grin.

'I knew you would.'

Mrs Shoutalot claps her hands and shouts.

'Right, children. Face this way. We're going to find out what you did in the summer holidays.'

Hands shoot up, Lucinda's first.

'Lucinda, you can begin.'

Mrs Shoutalot is what Dontie called my new teacher when he was in her class. Her real name is Mrs Sharratt but Mrs Shoutalot suits her better because she has a very loud voice.

We go around the class. It takes a LONG time to hear what everybody did in the summer holidays. Some people went away and some people stayed at home but half-way around, they all begin to sound the same. I yawn. It's warm in the

classroom. My eyelids start to droop.
Next to me, Lucinda is gently snoring.

'And last, but not least...!' booms
Mrs Shoutalot, extra-loud to get our
attention. My eyes shoot open as
twenty-three bodies sit bolt upright.
'Mattie! What did you do, my dear?'

I stand up. Twenty-two pairs of eyes
glaze over again; twenty-two bodies
slump. No one is interested any more.

I take a deep breath and tell the class
all about our holiday in Cornwall and
some of the people we came across.

I tell them about Ted whose farm we
stayed on.

I tell them about the beach called Sunset
Cove where we played every day.

I tell them about Cormoran, the giant
who lived in a castle and ate live sheep

and cows for breakfast, and some people open their eyes.

I tell them about the spriggans who steal babies from their cots and some people sit up and look interested.

I tell them about the knockers, the little faery people who look after you if you give them something to eat. I tell them how I saved my last piece of pizza for the knockers and they brought us Jellico, our dog, who had got left behind.

'Tell us more, Mattie,' says Joby, who's always told off for not listening.

I tell them about the silkies who look like seals, but some say are mermaids and mermen and some say are ghosts.

Now everyone is paying attention.

I tell them about Will, the friend I made, who had been trapped underground when the tin-mine collapsed a hundred years earlier.

Now everyone is sitting on the edge of their seats.

I tell them how my brother Dontie fell off a cliff and hurt his head and he would have drowned only Will led him to safety through a network of tunnels under the old tin-mine.

'And then, after that, Will turned back into a silkie and swam out to sea, to freedom,' I finish, and the whole class gasps.

'What next?' asks Joby.

'That's it,' I say. 'That's all that happened.'

'Well,' says Mrs Shoutalot, looking surprised. 'You've certainly got a vivid imagination, Mattie Butterfield.'

'Yes Miss,' I say and sit down.

But she's wrong. I haven't got a vivid imagination.

It's all true.

Chapter 3

Stanley takes to school like a duck to water.

After nearly three years, he hands the responsibility of looking after Anika back to Mum and goes off to school quite happily.

This surprises us all. You see, Anika was born on Stanley's second birthday.

'She's your birthday present, Stan,' Mum said when he saw her for the first time. She put the new baby into his arms.

'You've got to be a big boy now and look after your little sister. Can you do that for me?'

Stanley, who isn't a big boy at all, stared at brand new baby Anika, peeping up at him from her blanket, and nodded solemnly.

Stan is a man of his word.

Ever since, he has lugged Anika with him everywhere he goes. Anika is plump and cuddly like me and Stanley is small and skinny and every time Stanley sits down, she sits on his lap and he disappears.

You can't imagine one without the other. They are like:

 Jack and Jill

 Jelly and ice-cream

Batman and Robin

 Charlie and Lola

 Fish and chips

I thought Stanika would miss each other dreadfully. But here's the funny thing!

Anika's quite enjoying being left at home with Mum. Mum's got loads more time to spend with her now because the rest of us are all at school. And there's always Jellico for a cuddle if Mum's busy.

So that's one worry I can cross off my list. Anika can cope without Stan.

'It's not fair! I hate school,' says V, which is something she says a lot. 'I wish I could stay home with Mum.'

'We all feel like that sometimes,' I say

to cheer her up though, actually, I never want to stay home from school.

V scowls. 'I feel like that all the time.'

Meanwhile, Stanley absolutely loves school and doesn't seem to miss Anika at all while he's there. He's too busy learning to read.

Before long he is reading everything. Books, newspapers, magazines, comics; envelopes, letters, cereal boxes, food packets; road signs, shop signs, warning signs, **DO NOT** signs; notices, adverts, lists, receipts; bus timetables, train timetables, bills, leaflets...

I can't keep track of Stanley's reading.

One day, when Mum comes to collect us from school, Mr McGibbon, the reception class teacher, who is very tall with long arms, comes out with Stanley, who is very small with normal arms, to speak to her.

Mum looks alarmed. 'What's he done?'

'Young Stanley here is the best reader I have ever had,' announces Mr McGibbon.

Mum looks relieved. 'Is that all?'

'That, Mrs Butterfield, is everything.'

Mr McGibbon beams at us all.

Mum, Stanley, Anika and I beam back at him.

V studies her shoes.

So I can cross another worry off my list. Stan can cope without Anika.

Now I've only got one worry left. So I don't have much to worry about.

But here's another funny thing. Sometimes, when you've only got one worry, it looks even bigger and blacker on its own.

Now my list looks like this.

Worry List

 **1** V hates school.

Full stop.

Chapter 4

'Book!' says Anika as soon as we get home from school. 'Book. Book.'

She sounds like one of the chickens at Sunset Farm, scratching round the yard.

Anika has started saying lots of words since Stanley went to school.

'It's because Stanley's not around to speak for her,' says Grandma.

Grandma and Granddad were waiting for us at the door when we walked down the street. Mum went, 'Oh bother!'

when she saw them.

Actually Mum went 'Oh!' and another word but she wouldn't want me to repeat it.

It's not that Mum doesn't love Grandma and Granddad because she does.

I think.

She loves Granddad, definitely. I've heard her saying to Dad things like,

'Your father is a saint!'

And 'He deserves a medal, that man!'

And 'One day, he'll get his reward!'

Though she never says what for.

I think she loves Grandma too but sometimes I think she wishes she wouldn't interfere so much.

Grandma is good at interfering.

And winding people up.

And having her say.

And wanting her way.

And putting people straight.

And getting on her high-horse.

But Grandma is also good at lending a hand.

And tidying up.

And helping us with our vegetable patch.

And knitting us snuggly jumpers.

And making us delicious cakes.

And caring about us all.

I know, because I've heard Mum and Dad discussing Grandma.

A lot.

Soon we are all sitting round the kitchen table eating Grandma's chocolate cake and drinking orange squash (the children) and tea (the grown-ups) and listening to Stanley reading to Anika between bites of cake. It's one of Grandma's favourite books, *Peepo*.

'Here's a little baby, one two three...' recites Stanley solemnly and Anika and Grandma sit spellbound as he reads the whole book from cover to cover. When he gets to the end, they both smile with satisfaction.

'More?' says Anika hopefully.

'I love that book,' says Grandma. 'It reminds me of my childhood in wartime Britain. No waste then!'

Waste is one of Grandma's high-horses that she likes to perch on. She thinks we waste too much food because Stanley's a fussy eater and Dontie will eat chips but he won't eat fish and Anika will eat fish but she won't eat tomatoes and I will eat tomatoes but I won't eat Bolognese if there's meat in it.

In fact, I won't eat any meal if there's meat in it, even though I love all food. This is ever since we stayed at Sunset Farm and I realized that beef came from cows, and pork and bacon came from pigs, and lamb actually came from lamb, and chicken actually came from chicken.

'Just a phase,' Grandma had sniffed when Mum told her I was vegetarian. 'Tim went through that stage. She'll get over it.'

But she's wrong. Even if my dad did, I won't get over it. Ever.

Grandma approves of V's eating habits most because she'll eat anything, even though she's a skinny whippet. Grandma and V are alike in lots of ways, though

V can't knit snuggly jumpers or make delicious cakes.

But today, when Grandma says she loves *Peepo*, V snorts and rolls her eyes.

'What's up with you?' says Dontie and pokes her in the ribs.

'I hate that book,' says V. 'It's stupid.'

'No it isn't,' says Mum. 'Don't be rude.'

'All books are stupid!' says V.

'No they're not,' says Dontie. 'Just because you can't read.'

'Dontie!' warns Mum.

'Yes I can!' yells V. 'I just don't want to. It's stupid!'

'You're stupid!' says Dontie.

'Dontie!' snaps Mum, but it's too late.

V pushes him off his chair and runs off.

'Come back here V!' shouts Mum but I know she won't.

Because I saw tears rolling down her cheeks and she won't want anyone to know that she's crying.

Chapter 5

Mum is getting bigger and bigger. It's like someone's got hold of a balloon pump and blown up her tummy by mistake. Even though it's only October she starts getting ready for Christmas.

'Don't know what sort of state I'll be in by then,' she says. 'You'd better get your Christmas lists written nice and early this year, kids.'

We sit around the kitchen table with pens and paper.

Dontie scribbles down a big long list in two minutes flat, while I'm still thinking. Then he goes outside to kick a football around. I pick up the page and read it. It says:

 A pool table

 A Nintendo DS

 A surf board

 Computer games

 A new computer

 A mountain bike with accessories

 An iPod shuffle

 A zip-line

'Yeah, right,' says Mum, reading over my shoulder. 'I think Father Christmas might need a bigger sleigh.'

I rack my brains. Then I write:

 A hedgehog feeding station

 A wormery

 A flower press

 A chocolate-making kit

 Seeds for the vegetable patch

 A bat box

'A wormery!' shudders Mum. 'Where would you keep it?'

'You're not keeping it in the bedroom,' says V. 'It's my bedroom too and I'm **NOT** having worms in it.'

'I'd keep it in the garden,' I explain. 'Worms make lovely fertilizer.'

Stanley spends ages doing his list. It goes right down one side of the page and half-way down the other.

'What are you writing?' asks V who's just sitting there, doing nothing.

'A list of books with the titles in alphabetical order,' says Stanley, whose writing now is as good as his reading. 'To make it easier for Father Christmas. Did you know there's a book for each letter of the alphabet?'

'Big deal!' says V rudely. 'There are

twenty-six letters in the alphabet. That's loads. You're being greedy.'

'I don't want them all,' explains Stanley, hastily. 'He can choose.'

'Mouldy old books!' V wrinkles up her nose. 'I want a skateboard.'

'Write it down then,' says Mum.

V picks up a pen and hesitates. Then, with her tongue between her teeth, she slowly writes an S.

'That S is the wrong way round!' points out Stanley.

'Grr!' says V. 'I know that!' and she scribbles it out. Then she puts her pen down.

'Write it down!' repeats Mum. 'Or Father Christmas won't know what to bring you.'

'I only want one thing!' says V. 'He's

not going to forget that!'

'He's getting old,' says Mum. 'And he's got lots and lots of children to remember.'

V picks the pen back up reluctantly.

'Skateboard is easy to spell,' says Mum softly. 'S-K-...'

'...A-T-E...B-O-A-R-D,' continues Stanley helpfully.

'Don't tell me! I'm not stupid!' yells V and throws her pen down in a temper.

'Of course you're not,' says Mum, but it's too late, V's stormed out.

V's right. She's not stupid. She knows there are twenty-six letters in the alphabet.

It's just that she finds it hard to tell which one is which.

Chapter 6

'I've decided,' Grandma announces, 'this Christmas, I am going to cook the dinner.'

Oh no! Seven pairs of eyes look up at Grandma in alarm. Eight counting Jellico.

Every Christmas Day, Grandma, Granddad and Uncle Vesuvius come to us for Christmas dinner.

Uncle Vesuvius is Mum's foster dad. He's quite old and looks a bit like a garden gnome. I'm not being rude, it's true. He used to live with Aunty Etna, only she died, which is why he smokes a pen instead of a cigarette and comes to us for Christmas.

Mum and Dad cook the dinner between them. It's the best meal of the year because we all get to choose our favourite things to eat and then Mum and Dad put them all on the table and we can have what we like.

Mum says that when she was in the Children's Home all those years before she went to live with Uncle Vez and Aunty Etna she never got to choose what she ate. She just had to eat what was put in front of her.

So now Mum and Dad always cook a huge turkey with roast potatoes and carrots and sprouts and chestnut stuffing and lashings of gravy for the grown ups.

PLUS cheeseburger and chips, V's favourite, curry and rice, Dontie's favourite, and golden stars for Stanika. Golden stars are Dad's own, personal invention. It's cheese on toast cut into star shapes.

And for afters, there's Christmas pudding with brandy sauce or trifle or posh ice-creams or chocolate gateau.

I usually have a bit of everything.

Only this year, now I'm vegetarian, I won't be able to have the turkey. My favourite.

'But...' says Mum.

'No buts!' interrupts Grandma. 'You know it makes sense, Mona.'

To my surprise, Dad nods. 'Mum's right. You need to put your feet up this year, sweetheart. The baby will be due around then.'

Mum looks at us all, pleading at her silently with our eyes.

Her tummy ripples alarmingly as the baby kicks and does a handstand, and her eyes close.

'Thank you,' she says, when she opens them again. 'That's a very kind offer.'

'Good!' says Grandma, looking triumphant but surprised, like she was expecting Mum to put up more of a fight. 'That's settled then.'

'What are we having?' asks V who loves her food.

'Roast turkey with all the trimmings,' says Grandma. 'And Christmas pudding, of course.'

'What about cheeseburger and chips?' says V.

'And curry and rice?' asks Dontie.

'And Golden Stars?' asks Stanley.

Grandma clicks her tongue in

annoyance. 'There will be none of that eat-what-you-like-nonsense this year,' she says firmly. 'You're all old enough to eat what's put on your plate.'

'I won't eat sprouts,' says Dontie mutinously.

'That's enough,' says Grandma and Dontie flops down in a sulk.

'I don't like green beans,' says Stanley nervously. 'Neither does Anika.'

'I said that's enough, Stanley. You and Anika will eat what you're given.'

'But Grandma!' I say bravely. 'I'm vegetarian.'

'Vegetarian!' says Grandma and she looks as if she's going to explode. 'I'll give you vegetarian!'

And that, as far as Grandma is concerned, is the end of the matter.

Chapter 7

We are growing our Christmas dinner in the garden.

How cool is that?

Not all of it, obviously. You can't grow turkey or Christmas pudding in the garden.

But we have grown carrots and potatoes and sprouts!

The carrots that Stanika grew are already picked and washed and in our freezer.

The sprouts are still growing in our garden. I planted them! Did you know that Brussels sprouts grow on a big stalk above the ground, clinging on tight, like tiny baby cabbage monkeys?

I check them nearly every day. They're not ready yet.

'They'll be just right for Christmas,' says Uncle Vez, when he inspects them.

Uncle Vez is so clever. Guess what he's done! He's harvested the new potatoes, put some in compost in last Christmas's Chocolate and Cream Assorted Biscuits tin, and buried them in our garden.

'Keep nice and fresh they will. Taste 'andsome with sprouts and carrots and roast turkey on Christmas Day,' he says, smacking his lips at the prospect. 'Just the ticket!'

So Christmas dinner's all sorted.

But I'm a bit worried. What am I going to eat?

I can't eat turkey any more. Not since I've discovered it's … turkey.

I put it on my Worry List under 'V hates school' and it stays there for a while. Festering.

That means it's like a sore that doesn't get better. Instead it sort of keeps on oozing out.

In the end I talk to Lucinda about it because Mrs Shoutalot says that Lucinda has got an answer for everything.

She's right.

'Easy-peasy,' says Lucinda. 'Eat nut-roast instead. That's what my mum does. She's vegetarian. When she remembers.'

'What's nut roast?'

Lucinda thinks for a while. 'It's made of nuts. And it's roasted in the oven. It looks like meatloaf.'

'Sounds nice,' I say to be polite because she's been so helpful. But it doesn't really.

Anyway, when I ask Grandma if we can have nut roast for Christmas dinner she looks as if I've asked her if we can have slug-and-snail-roast with all the trimmings, and frogspawn-with-brandy-butter for afters. Her eyes go all big and poppy like she's about to internally combust.

'**NUT ROAST!**' she roars. '**NUT ROAST!!!!**'

I guess that means no.

Chapter 8

Stanley has won a prize for reading in school. It's a book, which is exactly the right prize for someone who's a good reader.

It's like a good footballer winning a football. Or a good cyclist winning a bike. Or a good swimmer winning a swimming pool. Much better than a certificate.

Mrs Dunnet, our headteacher, presented it to him in assembly and everyone clapped. Stanley shook hands with her and grinned from ear to ear. I felt really proud of my little brother.

Actually, one person didn't clap.

V.

She was sitting cross-legged on the floor of the hall two rows in front of me. She didn't even look up. She was hunched over with her elbows on her knees and her hands covering her ears like she didn't want to hear what was going on.

Later on, at lunchtime, I see her sitting outside her classroom on the naughty chair. I was in Miss Pocock's class last year and she never puts people on the naughty chair.

After school, V comes up behind me in the playground and grabs me by the arm.

'Come on!' she says urgently, 'Mum's waiting. She's in a hurry.'

I glance over at Mum waiting just inside the gate with Anika in the buggy. She's talking and laughing with lots of other mums. They remind me of the hens in the farmyard on holiday, heads going this way and that, clucking away to each other.

She doesn't look as if she's in a hurry. She looks as if she's having a nice time.

V looks a bit desperate. I turn around to see what's bothering her.

Miss Pocock is on duty in the yard.

Stanley runs up to Mum and shows her his prize.

'Well done!' she says in delight and all the mums start squawking together at the same time.

'Clever boy! Cluck. Clever Stanley! Cluck, cluck. Aren't you a clever boy?

Cluck, cluck, cluck.'

'We need to go! Now!' says V, interrupting. Miss Pocock is walking towards us.

'What's the rush?' says Mum in surprise.

'I've got homework to do.'

Mum raises her eyebrows at the other mums. 'Well I never! Better be off then! Bye everyone!'

'Bye-bye!' they all cluck. 'Well done, Stanley!'

V scowls and marches on ahead.

'She's keen!' says Mum, struggling to keep up with her. But after we've turned the corner, V slows down and soon she's lagging behind us, dragging her bag on the ground.

'Come on, slow-coach!' calls Mum, glancing back to see what she's up to.

'I thought you were in a rush to start your homework.'

'I'm not slow!' snaps V and shoots in front of us to prove it.

'That's better,' says Mum and smiles at her encouragingly. But then two minutes later, V has fallen behind again and is wandering along gloomily, head down, trailing her bag behind her and scuffing her toes in the dust.

'Come on, V!' says Mum, crossly this time. 'Pick your bag up. And your feet! You're ruining your new shoes.'

'I'm coming!' scowls V and flounces past, knocking Stanley flying.

'Mind Stanley!' shouts Mum as she grabs his arm to stop him from landing head-first in the road. But V ignores her and runs on home ahead of us.

'What's got into her?' grumbles Mum.

I know. And I'm just wondering whether to tell Mum or not when all of a sudden, she groans. 'Oh, no! That's all we need.'

Outside our house, Grandma and Granddad are getting out of their car.

Chapter 9

'I'll make the tea, you put your feet up,' instructs Grandma. Mum obeys wearily, sinking down onto a chair.

She looks worn out. It must be hard work if you think about it, carrying a baby round in your tummy and pushing a big sturdy toddler in a buggy at the same time.

And coping with V in a strop.

There's no sign of my sister. She's disappeared.

'V!' calls Mum. 'Where are you?'

No answer. Dontie walks in. 'She's lying on her bed, peeling off bits of wallpaper,' he says.

'V! Come down here!' shouts Mum.

Silence.

Mum looks rattled.

Anika goes to Stan and climbs onto his lap. Stan disappears.

Dontie whistles to himself.

Grandma pours the tea.

Mentally I add a new worry to my list in big, bold letters.

 V's going to get it!

Mum gets up, holding her back, and walks to the foot of the stairs.

'V!'

'What?'

My sister's voice sounds really grumpy.

'Come down here this minute. I'm not telling you again!'

'Drink your tea while it's hot,' says Grandma quietly. Mum sits back down again and takes a sip. She gives Stanley a little smile.

'Show Grandma and Granddad your prize, Stan.'

Stan wriggles out from under Anika and fetches his book for Grandma.

'What's this for?' she asks.

'Reading,' he says shyly.

'You clever boy! Look at this, Arnold! Our Stan's won a prize for reading.'

'He's a clever lad!' says Granddad. 'Let me see, Stanley.'

V comes in and slumps down at the

table next to Mum. She looks really moody.

'I thought you had homework to do,' says Mum.

'Done it,' says V.

'No you haven't!'

'Yes I have! It's only reading.'

'Let's hear it then.'

'No! I told you, I've done it.'

Mum looks as if she wants to slap V.

But she won't.

V looks as if she wants to slap Mum.

But she won't.

Granddad looks up from admiring Stanley's book. 'You'll never be a good reader like our Stan unless you practise your reading, V,' he says.

Mum closes her eyes.

'Reading's stupid!' says V which is what

she always says. 'Can I go now?'

'No!' says Mum. 'You can sit here till everyone else has done their homework.'

Dontie and I settle down to ours while Stanley reads Anika a story from his new book.

Then he reads one to Grandma and Granddad while Mum starts to cook tea.

Then, when Dad comes home, he reads one to him as well.

All the time, V sits there, arms folded, bottom lip out, cross as a crab, and doesn't say a word.

She eats up all her tea but she won't say goodbye to Grandma and Granddad when they go home.

She won't kiss Stanley goodnight either when he goes to bed. Or Anika.

She won't speak to me when we get into bed and she wriggles right away to the edge as far away from me as possible.

'What's up, V?' asks Mum when she comes to tuck us in. She kneels down by my sister's side of the bed and strokes her hair out of her eyes. 'You're not jealous of Stanley, are you?'

V jerks her head away. 'NO!' she says crossly. 'Stanley's stupid!'

'No, he's not,' Mum sighs. She doesn't sound mad at V any more, she just sounds very tired. 'Nobody's stupid. Now go to sleep.'

V doesn't go to sleep though. She pretends to, but I can tell she's not, because she keeps sniffing. After a while

I dare to put my arm around her. Then her sniffs turn to sobs and she turns around to cuddle into me.

'It's all right,' I say and pat her on the back.

But it isn't.

Chapter 10

It's magic in school coming up to Christmas. In Mrs Shoutalot's class we make angels out of bright, shiny foil and string them up around the classroom.

I take in some holly from the tree in the corner of our garden and Mrs Shoutalot is pleased and pins it up.

But then Joby brings in some mistletoe and chases the girls with it. He catches Lucinda and she squeals like mad and Mrs Shoutalot tells him off and confiscates the mistletoe.

He doesn't chase me even though I can't run as fast as Lucinda.

In Art we make Christmas cards and in Maths we make calendars and then we practise the play.

I'm the star.

Mum is very excited when I tell her I'm going to be the star of our Christmas show.

'Are you really!' she says and gives me a big squeeze. 'Well done, Mattie. Do you have a lot to say?'

'No, I don't say anything.'

'Oh, so you're singing, are you? You've got a lovely voice. No wonder Mrs Sharrat chose you.'

'No, I don't sing.'

'Do you dance?'

'No, I don't dance.'

Mum looks puzzled. 'What do you do then?'

'I stand there with my arms out, like this. See?' I demonstrate. 'Mrs Sharrat picked me because I'm good at standing still.'

'I see.' But I don't think she does because that little frown is there playing between her eyes, then she says, 'What part do you actually play, Mattie? Remind me again.'

'The star,' I say again, patiently. 'I'll need a costume.'

'It's a nativity play,' explains Dontie. 'Mrs Shoutalot's class always does the nativity play every year.'

'I have to stand completely still on a big wooden box so everyone can see me and find their way to the stable where Jesus is born.'

Mum's face clears and breaks into a huge smile. 'Oh, I see! You're the star!'

I stare at her blankly.

'That's what I said.'

At school we go to the hall to practise. More often than not, when we pass Miss Pocock's classroom, V is sitting outside on the naughty chair.

'Why is V so naughty?' whispers Lucinda to me.

'I don't know,' I whisper back.

Because V isn't always naughty. She can be really good.

She's good at sharing.

She's good at eating everything up without a fuss which is being really good in Grandma's book.

She's good at being neat and tidy and she makes our bed in the morning so we don't get told off because I always forget.

She's good at working out sums in her head like the price of our veggies when we sold them back in the summer.

She's good at getting up on time and going to bed on time and cleaning her teeth without being reminded and washing her hair on her own and all those other things that grown-ups think are important.

She's good at making us all laugh, and thinking up new games, and running fast, and playing cricket with Dontie, and playing baby games with Anika and listening to my Worry List.

In fact, personally, I think V likes being good.

But lately she's been really naughty.

And now I can't tell her my Worry List anymore, because it's all about her.

It looks like this.

Worry List

1 Why is V always sitting on the naughty chair at school?

2 Why is she not very nice at home?

3 Especially to Stanley?

4 Why does she cry herself to sleep at night?

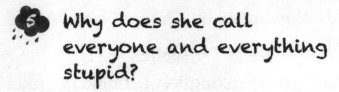 Why does she call everyone and everything stupid?

 Why won't she/can't she read?

Chapter 11

One day Mrs Dunnet comes out of school and asks Mum if she can have a word with her in her office.

'Yes, of course,' shrills Mum, smiling at my head teacher. 'Wait here girls and look after Anika for me. Come on, Stanley.'

Poor Mum. She thinks it's about Stanley doing well.

It isn't. It's about V not doing well.

V has been sitting outside Mrs Dunnet's office all day. She even had her lunch there.

Mrs Dunnet coughs. 'Actually, it's Vera Lynn I want to talk to you about, Mrs Butterfield.'

Mum glances down at V in surprise. V looks as if she's shrivelled to about a third of her size.

'Right,' says Mum and her voice sounds flat now. 'Mattie, you're in charge. Come with me, V.'

Mum and V are in Mrs Dunnet's office for a long time. A very long time. During that time:

Mr McGibbon comes out, gets on his bike and cycles away.

Mrs Shoutalot comes out and shouts, 'What are you still doing here?' Then she gets in her car and drives off, without waiting for an answer.

Miss Pocock comes out, glances guiltily

in our direction, and scuttles off out of the gate as fast as she can.

Stanley gets bored.

Anika gets hungry.

I get worried.

More teachers drive off in their cars.

The caretaker comes out and stares at us.

Then he stares at his watch.

Then he rattles his keys.

And at last, Mum comes out with V.

V looks as if she's shrivelled up even more.

Mum looks hot and bothered.

We walk home without a word. Dad comes home and Mum disappears into the kitchen with him to make tea while we sit at the table doing our homework. Snatches of Mum's voice come floating through the closed door.

'Can't read ... won't try ... She says she's lazy ... disruptive ... cheeky ... falling behind ... Such a disappointment ... not like the others ... little Stanley doing so well ... Could it be the new baby? **BLOOMING CHEEK!**'

As Mum's voice gets higher and higher, V's cheeks get pinker and pinker. For the first time ever, she buries her nose in a book. But I can't help noticing, she doesn't turn the pages.

From the other side of the kitchen door we can hear Dad's voice calming Mum down.

'Don't upset yourself ... not good for the baby ... I'll have a word ... now don't you worry...'

V has very good hearing. She doesn't

miss a thing.

At tea no one says very much. Jellico lies with his head on his paws winking at us but no one responds. After tea, Mum and Dad wash up.

Then Dad clears his throat. 'We're going to put Stanika to bed, then Mum and I would like a word with you, V. In private.'

V doesn't answer.

'Oh,' says Stanley, disappointed. I glance at the clock. Poor Stanley. It's very early for his bedtime.

'Don't worry, old chap,' says Dad. 'You can read your Reading Prize book for a while in bed.'

'Yay!' says Stanley and throws his arms in the air like he's scored a goal and Jellico barks. Mum and Dad laugh and suddenly everything seems back to normal. Almost.

But then V makes a rude snorting noise in her nose.

Dad looks at her. 'What's that for?' he asks. Everything goes silent. Jellico creeps under the table.

'I said, what's that silly noise for?'

'Stanley,' says V, and she rolls her eyes. 'He's so stupid!'

Stanley's face falls.

'No, he isn't,' says Dad.

'Yes he is,' says V mutinously and her face goes dark.

'No, he isn't,' repeats Dad, getting cross. 'You're st—'

'Tim!' warns Mum but it's too late. V jumps to her feet and shoots past us all and up the stairs. Dad bites his lip.

He stopped himself in time but everyone knew what he was going to say.

Including V.

Chapter 12

Mum puts Anika to bed.

Stanley gets himself washed, puts on his pyjamas and brushes his teeth.

Dontie flops down beside me on the sofa.

'Night-night,' says Stanley, and gives us all a hug. Then he takes himself off upstairs, scrubbed and pink and clean, looking forward to reading his book in bed.

Dad sighs deeply and gets to his feet.

'Right then. I suppose I'd better go and have a word with that sister of yours.'

But then the door bell rings and I jump up to look out of the front room window.

'It's Grandma and Granddad!'

'Great!' says Dad weakly but he doesn't sound as if he means it. I run to the front door to let them in.

'What a nice quiet house!' says Grandma as she steps into the hall. But then from upstairs comes **ONE ALMIGHTY HOWL**...

... the Loudest, Scariest, most Blood-Curdling **HOWL** you have ever heard in your whole life. It fills the house.

Jellico's hair stands on end and he streaks straight out of the open front door, right through Grandma's legs.

Mum and Dad burst out of the front room. 'What's going on?' asks Dad.

We all stand in the hall where the Enormous Howl is being replaced by Enormous Shouting and Bawling.

Now we can hear Anika starting to cry in her bedroom as she's torn from sleep, while outside Jellico is barking and yelping and growling.

'What on earth...?' says Mum. She starts to climb the stairs, then comes to a halt. 'Stanley!' she gasps. 'Whatever's the matter?'

My little brother has appeared at the top, heaving and blowing and gulping for air. He's clutching his prize book to his chest and is in floods of tears.

'Look!' he shrieks and opens his book. Loose pages float down the stairs. One

lands on my foot. I pick it up and catch my breath. Someone has scribbled all over it.

Behind him V appears, her face wet and streaming and covered in snot.

'I'm sorry! I'm sorry! I'm sorry!' she yells.

'Oh Vera Lynn!' groans Grandma. 'What have you done?'

But she doesn't sound cross.

She sounds sad.

Chapter 13

This is the worst day of my life.

Definitely.

It's even worse than the day Dontie fell down the cliff because I knew that Will was helping me then.

Today my Worry List has grown legs and leapt off the page and run around our house causing chaos.

This is the day I've always been afraid of. I thought if I wrote it down, it wouldn't happen.

I was wrong. It just did.

I look at Stanley, his torn-up, scribbled-out, prize book dangling from his hand, pages floating to the floor. His mouth is wide-open, his eyes are tight-shut, and he's started howling again.

I have never seen Stanley so upset.

I look at V standing next to him, moaning and shuddering, while huge tears course down her cheeks.

I have never seen V so distraught.

I look at my parents, round-eyed with surprise.

They don't know what to do!

Then Grandma takes charge.

'Never mind, Stanley!' She takes one, two, three giant steps to the top of the stairs (I didn't know she could move so fast!) and scoops him up. 'There, there, now,' she says, patting him on the back, 'Don't you worry, little man. We can get you another book. Here you are, Tim.'

Dad reaches up for him and she dumps my little brother into his arms.

Then she picks up the sobbing V and says, 'That's quite enough for now, young lady,' and carries her into our bedroom. The door shuts firmly behind them.

It turns out to be a very late bedtime for everyone.

I can't go to bed, because Grandma's in my bedroom talking to V and Stanley can't go to bed because he's upset.

So Mum and Dad let us all stay up and watch the telly for a treat, even Anika. Anika thinks it's lovely.

'We're not making a habit of this!' mutters Mum as the clock ticks by and

Anika shows no signs of closing her eyes.

At last a door opens upstairs. Eight pairs of eyes, including Jellico's, watch as V and Grandma come downstairs, hand in hand, and stand in front of us.

'V has something she would like to say,' Grandma says and switches the television off. No one complains, not even Dontie.

V, head down, walks over to Stanley who is sitting on Dad's lap. When she lifts her face up to look at him, it's all blotchy and her eyes are red and swollen. But at least she's stopped shuddering.

'I'm sorry, Stan, I'm really sorry!' she says and once more, tears spill out of her eyes and roll down her cheeks. 'I'll never do such a dreadful thing again, I promise. I'm going to buy you a new book tomorrow.'

'How?' I say, puzzled. I know for a fact that V hasn't got any money. She spends all her pocket money as soon as she gets it.

'I'm going to lend V the money,' explains Grandma. 'And she's going to pay it back to me every week out of her pocket money. Starting tomorrow.'

'That'll take years!' gasps Dontie.

'It'll take a few weeks,' says Grandma.

'I don't mind,' hiccups V. 'I'm really sorry, Stan.'

Stan reaches out and puts his arms round her neck. 'That's all right, V.'

V starts crying again in earnest.

Anika wriggles off Mum's knee and stands next to V. Then she stretches up on tip-toe to very gently touch a tear on her sister's cheek. I don't think she's ever seen

V cry before.

V in a strop, yes. V in floods of tears, no.

'Drips!' says Anika, fascinated.

'No,' explains Stanley. 'Tears.'

'Drips!' insists Anika, prodding V's face again.

'Tears,' says Stanley, patiently.

'Drips!' persists Anika, sticking to her guns.

V makes a funny noise and starts shuddering again.

'Tears!' says Stan, louder.

'Drips!' says Anika, louder still. She points to one on the end of V's nose and pats it. Hard.

'Ow!' says V.

'Tears!' shouts Stanley.

'DRIPS!' roars placid little Anika.

Grandma makes a funny noise too, same as V. Oh no! I don't believe it! Grandma is going to start crying as well.

I look to Mum for help.

Something strange is happening to my family.

Mum's shaking.

Dad's groaning.

V's shuddering.

Grandma's convulsing.

Granddad's shoulders are heaving.

Dontie's fallen off the sofa and is thrashing about on the floor.

What's wrong with everyone?

Oh, I get it!

'No, Stanley. Drips!' announces Anika.

And everyone bursts out laughing, including V, as Anika, in the first sentence of her life, wins the argument.

Anika beams at us all.

'Drips,' she repeats with satisfaction. 'Drips.'

Chapter 14

On Saturday, Grandma takes V shopping to buy a new book for Stanley. Dontie goes out to meet his new mates from secondary school. Mum and Dad take Stanika to the park but I stay home with Granddad. I need to think about Christmas presents.

I sit at the table and make a list. I'm good at making lists. I just think about what everyone likes best and write it down. It looks like this.

MUM: A great big bunch of flowers

 DAD: Some new paints

 DONTIE: A Nintendo DS

 V: Skateboard stuff

 STANLEY: A book

 ANIKA: Same as Stanley

Brilliant!

I go upstairs, open my money box and count out the coins.

It comes to £1.73p.

I come downstairs again.

'Granddad?'

'Mmm?' Granddad is reading the paper.

'How much is a Nintendo?'

'A Nin-what-o?'

'Never mind.' I know I don't have enough. I sigh deeply.

Granddad peers at me over the top of the paper. 'What's up, Mattie?'

'I'm writing my Christmas present list for everyone and there's a problem.'

'What's that?'

'I don't think I can afford to buy them.'

'Don't worry about me,' he says cheerfully. 'I don't want one.'

Oops. I forgot. I add two more names to the list.

GRANDDAD

GRANDMA

There's a knock on the front door and then it's pushed open to reveal Uncle Vez.

Oh dear.

I add another name to the list.

 ## UNCLE VESUVIUS

Then I remember someone else.

 ## LUCINDA

'Homework?' asks Uncle Vez.

'No, I'm making a list of people I've got to get Christmas presents for.'

'That's a lot of people,' says Uncle Vez, peering over my shoulder.

'But there's a problem,' explains Granddad. 'No cash.'

'That's always the problem. Never mind, it's the thought that counts,' says Uncle Vez. 'Cross me off.'

I draw a line through his name. Then I

draw a line through Granddad's.

'But,' I say, thoughtfully, 'even if I cross you and Granddad off my list...'

'And Grandma, and your dad and your mum. They won't want one,' interrupts Granddad. I draw a line through Mum's and Dad's and Grandma's names.

'Yes, but...' I do a quick count and sigh. 'That's still one-two-three-four-five presents I've got to buy. Because if I give Dontie or V or Stanika or Lucinda a present and they unwrap it and it's an empty box and I say, "It's the thought that counts," I think they might be a bit disappointed.'

'Mmm, I see where you're coming from,' concedes Granddad.

'Best kind of presents are the ones you make yourself,' remarks Uncle Vez.

'True,' says Granddad. 'Got any ideas?'

'Plenty,' says Uncle Vez. 'Have you still got those pebbles you brought back from Sunset Cove?'

'Yes! They're in my bedroom!'

'Go and fetch 'em down, then. We'll be out in the shed.'

Oh my goodness! The **VERY** best kind of presents are the ones your granddad and your great uncle help you to make. They are amazing! But everyone is going to have to wait till Christmas Day to find out what they are.

Anyway, they're finished, wrapped up neatly and hiding under my bed ready for Christmas by the time the others come home. I hug my secret to myself like a hot water bottle.

'What have you been up to, Mattie?'

asks Mum.

'Oh, nothing much,' I say airily and cross my fingers because it's a lie. A white lie. Granddad winks at me and Uncle Vez puts his hands in his pockets, stares up at the ceiling and whistles innocently to himself.

'You should've come with us,' says Mum. 'I thought Grandma and V would be home by now. I wonder where they've got to?'

Grandma and V don't come home till nearly teatime.

And when V walks in everyone gasps!

Chapter 15

V is wearing glasses!

She doesn't half look different! Not so fierce, and older and wiser, like a little skinny owl, minus the feathers.

'Look at you!' shrieks Mum. 'They suit you, V!'

'You look like a little intellectual,' agrees Dad, grinning broadly.

'What's an intellectual?' asks Stanley.

'A clever person. Don't you think your sister looks clever, Stan?'

Stanley nods solemnly, gazing at V as if he's not quite sure he recognizes her.

'Me?' squeals Anika and reaches up for V's new glasses. 'My go?'

V shakes her head. 'No Anika, they're not for playing with. They're to help me see better.'

'Do they work?' I ask. V's face lights up.

'They're brilliant! Everything is bright and clear and shiny now, like new. Things aren't foggy any more.'

Mum gulps. 'Oh dear, I never knew things were foggy, V,' she says and she sounds a bit ashamed as if she should've known.

Because, come to think of it, Mum knows pretty much everything about us.

'Neither did I,' says V simply. 'Until I got my glasses.'

'When did you realize?' asks Dad, turning to Grandma.

'Only recently. I wasn't sure, it was just a hunch. We had a good talk last night, didn't we?'

V nods. 'I told Grandma I hated school because everyone else can read except for me.' Her little face behind her new glasses looks stricken. 'That's why I was so angry with you, Stanley. Because you can read so well and I can't. Even though I'm older.'

'Is that why you scribbled on my book and tore it up?'

V nods sadly. 'I'm sorry.'

'She's such a bright little thing, there had to be a reason why she couldn't read,' says Grandma. 'And she was behaving so badly I thought it was time to get to the bottom of it before she turned into a juvenile delinquent.'

'What's a juvenile delinquent?' asks Stanley.

'Someone with an ASBO,' explains Dontie.

'What's someone with an "asbo"?' Stanley asks a lot of questions nowadays.

'Someone who doesn't know how to behave themselves,' says Dad. 'So you took her to have her eyes tested? Genius!'

'Well, I thought it wouldn't do any harm. And bingo! It turns out, that's what all the trouble was about. The poor child couldn't see beyond the end of her nose.'

Poor V. She's only got a little nose.

'Now, with my new glasses, I can see that all the letters are different. I couldn't tell before,' says V proudly.

'Well I never!' says Uncle Vez, puffing on his biro. 'Maybe I should get meself a new pair of specs. I might turn out to be Brain of Britain!'

'Here's your new book, Stanley.' V hands it over to him.

'You can read it first,' says Stanley generously.

'No, it's OK, I haven't learned yet,' says V. 'But I will soon.'

I am so happy V is sorted out. Everyone is.

At this rate I can throw away my Worry List.

Good old Grandma.

Chapter 16

It's Christmas Eve Night.

My favourite night of the year.

Stanika are already tucked up in bed.

V is curled up reading. Two weeks, that's all it took for her to learn to read.

'She's always got her nose stuck in a book, that girl,' complains Mum, but she's got smiley eyes so she doesn't mean it. Well, she does mean it, but she doesn't mind.

V is reading her way through all the

books she can find, making up for lost time. Once she could see the letters, she was fine. She still makes mistakes though. Like tonight, she was reading Anika her bedtime story and she said, 'So, Peter was missled and—'

'What's missled?' asked Stanley. 'Is it like whistled?'

'Um … I don't know but that's what it says here.'

Stanley took a look. 'That word is mis-led.'

V looked at it again. 'Oh yeah,' she said and carried right on reading the story.

Three weeks ago she would've stomped off in a temper if Stanley had pointed out she'd made a mistake.

Actually, three weeks ago she wouldn't have been reading a story in the first place.

I can't wait to see everyone's faces when they get their present from me tomorrow. I've been so scared that someone would discover them under my bed. Luckily, V is not the sort of person to look under a bed to see if there is something or someone lurking there (not like me!) so they've been safe.

But ... I'm worried.

I don't want to be worried on Christmas Eve but I can't help it.

I've got a Worry List with two things on it.

Two things. Actually, that's not many. I've had loads more than that in the past.

This is my Christmas Worry List:

 Sprouts

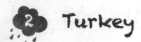 Turkey

1 The sprouts

I promised Grandma sprouts for our Christmas dinner.

I planted them back in the summer and they were doing so well. But now something's gone wrong.

The leaves have gone yellow and wizened. Uncle Vez says they've 'blown' which I think means they've opened up and they don't look very nice. Uncle Vez keeps muttering things like 'cabbage fly', and 'root maggot', and 'pesky little grubs', and now no one wants to eat them any more.

Dontie's pleased because he doesn't like sprouts anyway but I'm mortified.

I promised!

Before he went home, Uncle Vez said,

'Leave it till tomorrow Mattie and we'll see what they look like in the morning.'

But they're not going to get better overnight, are they?

2 The turkey

Grandma says she's going to do a Christmas dinner for us to remember. She's doing it all, the whole thing.

She's bought a posh Christmas table cloth with holly on it and proper napkins to match.

She's bought good quality crackers, not rubbish ones, with real presents inside like pencil sharpeners and tiny packs of cards and combs and hair slides. I hope I get a hair slide.

She's bought a ceramic Father Christmas on his sleigh with all his reindeer for the centre of the table, and Rudolph's got a flashing nose.

She's bought sparkling wine and fizzy pop to drink with our dinner, plus whisky for Granddad and Dad and Uncle Vesuvius and a bottle of sherry for herself.

She's made mince pies and a Christmas pudding with silver coins in it, and brandy butter and cranberry sauce, and she's coming back in the morning to do chestnut stuffing and pigs in blankets and the veg.

The turkey is sitting in the roasting tin on our cooker, waiting to go in the oven.

'All under control,' she said with satisfaction, taking one last look round before she went home. 'You, Mona, are not lifting a finger tomorrow!'

Mum, who was sitting on the sofa with

her feet up, grabbed Grandma's hand as she went past and said, 'Bless you,' and Grandma went all pink.

I think Mum and Grandma like each other now.

All this is good. Really good. But the problem is:

Grandma says Christmas without turkey is like:

 tea without milk

 bread without butter

 gin without tonic

And I think she's forgotten I'm a vegetarian.

Chapter 17

In our house Father Christmas comes down the chimney and leaves our big presents out on display in the centre of the living room.

He leaves our smaller presents wrapped up with labels on the chairs.

This Christmas, in the middle of the room, he has left:

 A mountain bike

 A skateboard

A bright-red school
desk with a seat
attached to it

 A baby doll in a pram

 A wooden box with
a roof and a door
in the front of it

'Wow!' says Dontie, his eyes on the
bike. 'Is that for me?'

'Well, the doll and pram isn't, that's
for sure!' grins Dad. 'And I think it's too
big for everyone else. Unless it's for me?'

'No way!' shouts Dontie and jumps
on the bike. 'Thanks, Father Christmas!'

'Now you'll be able to ride to school
with your friends,' says Mum.

'A skateboard!' yells V and leaps
straight on to it. The board upends and
she lands on her bottom. 'Ouch!'

'I'll show you how to do it,' says Dontie. 'What have you got, Mattie? A bird table?'

'It's a bat-box!' I say in delight. 'Just what I wanted!'

'Good,' says Mum and she laughs as Anika peers inside the pram and pulls the baby doll out by one leg. 'Gently, Anika. You've got to look after babies

very carefully.'

'That doll's pram is just like the one I had when I was little!' I say in surprise.

'Well I never, so it is,' says Dad. 'Father Christmas must have a stock of them.' He and Mum exchange an amused look.

'I wonder what happened to it?' says Mum. 'V was never a doll-and-pram sort of girl.'

She takes Anika's doll in her arms and shows her how to cradle it properly. Anika beams and snatches it off her, rocking it at top speed like a tiny, turbo-charged, mini-mum.

I think she's definitely going to be a doll-and-pram sort of girl.

'Is that for me?' asks Stanley, staring at the desk, wide-eyed. Dad nods and squats down beside it as Stanley cautiously sits and lifts the lid.

'I had one like this when I was a boy,' explains Dad. 'Only mine wasn't red, it was just plain wood. I used to sit at it to read and write and draw. I'd keep all my drawing stuff and my favourite books in it, nice and safe. Look, you can even lock it up with this little key.'

Stanley practises locking and unlocking

his desk. Then he opens his presents on the chair and finds he has lots of new books to put inside.

All Christmas morning he sits there at his desk, silently reading his way through his Christmas books, while the rest of us open our presents around him and rush in and out of the house trying them out.

I pop my new seeds and fork and trowel into the shed. There's an empty pot of paint on the worktop. That's funny. It's exactly the same shade as Stanley's desk.

My presents! I almost forgot. I run upstairs and come down with them in my arms.

'One for you, one for you, one for you, one for you!' I give them out, one each to my brothers and sisters. Mum and Dad look on as they tear off the wrapping paper and inspect the contents.

'What is it?' asks V looking puzzled.

Enclosed in a small cage made of balsa wood, a smooth, grey pebble stares back at her, unblinking, its round eyes made from stuck-on buttons and beads.

'It's Petroc. Your own pet rock. Get it?'

'Wicked!' laughs Dontie. 'A pet rock! I like it.'

'You don't have to feed it or clean it or take it for a walk,' I explain. 'You just have to talk to it and take it out of its cage

114

every so often and give it a cuddle.'

'Cool!' says V. 'It's my best present ever!' She pops it into her pocket and whizzes off out of the door on her new skateboard which she's now got the hang of.

Crash!

Nearly.

Grandma and Granddad have arrived.

Chapter 18

Christmas Day has been brilliant up to this point, but now I have to face the two items on my Worry List which are:

 Will my sprouts be all right to eat?

 Will Grandma make me eat the turkey? (Which I want to but I can't, now I'm a vegetarian.)

Dad popped the turkey into the oven when he got up this morning and now all Grandma has to do is put the veg on.

'Can you go and pick your sprouts for me, Mattie love?' she asks, slipping the pigs in blankets and the stuffing into the hot oven.

I've been dreading this moment. I hate letting people down. I take the bowl she offers me, feeling sure that my sprouts won't be good enough to eat.

The door opens. Uncle Vesuvius comes in, carrying last Christmas's Chocolate and Cream Assorted Biscuits tin with the new potatoes in it and a big net bag.

'Here you are, Mattie. I picked your sprouts for you on my way in.'

I peep inside. 'They look all right!' I say in surprise.

'Came good in the end after all,' he says. 'Sprouts do that sometimes.'

'Pity!' groans Dontie.

But I am delighted.

Then we all open our presents from Grandma and Granddad and Uncle Vesuvius and I get a flower press and a chocolate-making set from Grandma and Granddad and a hedgehog-feeding station from Uncle Vez, so apart from my wormery (which can wait 'til another day, there's no rush), I get everything I wanted.

V gets lots and lots of books from Grandma and Granddad and guess what?

She's really pleased.

Then we all have Christmas cocktails with straws and little umbrellas.

'Don't get me tipsy,' giggles Mum. 'Not in my condition.'

She looks a bit tipsy. Her cheeks are

very pink and she's puffing and blowing a bit.

Before long, Grandma says, 'Right then, you lot, dinner is served!' and we all sit down at the table and pull crackers and I do get a hair-slide in mine and V reads out everyone's joke. It's brilliant fun.

But then, Grandma places dish after dish after dish on the table and I go quiet. And still. This is the second moment I've been dreading.

For Christmas dinner we have:

 glazed carrots

 Brussels sprouts with sautéed chestnuts

 new potatoes, dripping in butter

 sizzling roast potatoes

yummy chipolatas wrapped in bacon blankets

 balls of stuffing packed with apricots, celery and chestnuts

 steaming hot jugs of bread sauce and gravy

 cranberry sauce

 ... and a delicious-smelling, rich dark-brown turkey

But I can't eat it.

The turkey, that is. Nor the pigs in blankets. Grandma's going to be so disappointed.

It's sooooo hard being a vegetarian.

'Well,' gasps Mum, studying the laden table. 'Marjorie, you have done us proud!'

'I've not finished yet,' says Grandma and she comes back in carrying one last dish. 'It's the first time I've tried it, so I don't know what it will taste like.'

'What is it?' asks V.

'Nut roast,' says Grandma.

It tastes delicious.

Chapter 19

I love Christmas Day. You eat and eat and eat until you are totally stuffed.

After dinner, Mum says, 'Do you know, I think I might have a lie-down.'

She looks totally stuffed, but actually, I couldn't help noticing, she hardly ate a thing. She kept slipping bits of her turkey breast to Jellico even though she never lets us feed him at the table. And she left all her vegetables.

Grandma noticed too, but she didn't

tell her off like she would if it was one of us.

I think she knows there's nowhere left for the food to go in Mum's tummy. The baby's taking up all the room.

Dad gives Mum a hand upstairs.

'All hands on deck!' booms Uncle Vesuvius and we all help with the washing up except for Anika and Jellico who have fallen asleep on the mat together in front of the fire and Grandma, because she was the cook.

I scrape the plates into the bin on top of the net bag Uncle Vez collected the sprouts in. It's got a Tesco label on it. Then I make Grandma a nice cup of tea while Granddad clears the table, Uncle Vez washes up, Dontie dries and V and Stanley put away.

V tries to do this on her skateboard but it doesn't work. She crashes into the cupboard and smashes Grandma's best gravy jug. Grandma makes her put her skateboard outside.

When everything is tidy, Granddad pours Uncle Vez and himself a drop of whisky and Grandma a sweet sherry and then they sit down in front of the telly to listen to the Queen's speech.

But her speech can't be very good because, in no time at all, they are all fast asleep and snoring their heads off.

'Let's go out to play,' says V who's desperate to get back on her skateboard.

Outside, Dontie sets up an obstacle course for his new mountain bike and V's new skateboard. He has lots of obstacles to choose from.

Most people don't have stone

dinosaurs

fairies

owls

helicopters

angels

Batman

kangaroos

eagles

dragons

racing cars

cats, dogs
and goats

a penguin

daleks

gnomes

turtles   Superman

praying mantis

                    ghosts
dolphins

              hedgehogs
spaceships

              cherubs

    sharks   tractors

digger trucks

and **polar bears** in their garden.
But we do.

My dad's a sculptor as well as an artist.

Every birthday he makes us a new sculpture and we get to choose whatever we want.

Dad pops his head out of the bedroom window to watch us playing in the garden. I give him a wave and call out, 'Dad! We'll need another sculpture soon for the new baby.'

He looks back inside the bedroom for a second and then his face reappears, smiling.

'Yep, I think you're right there, Mattie love,' he says.

From the bedroom window comes a groan.

Chapter 20

The midwife arrives with her bag around teatime just as it's getting dark.

'Hi kids!' she says. 'Father Christmas been?' But she disappears upstairs with Dad without waiting for an answer.

'Can I go up to see Mum?' asks V but Grandma won't let her.

We have Christmas cake and trifle but no one is that hungry.

We watch television but no one is that interested.

We play charades but no one is concentrating.

The clock ticks on. And on. And on.

Granddad and Uncle V grow quieter and quieter.

Grandma grows twitchier and twitchier.

Dontie grows fidgety.

V grows grumpy.

Stanika grow tired.

I grow worried.

Then I have an idea.

I nip out to the kitchen and open the fridge door as quietly as I can.

I peel a bit of turkey from the carcass and put it on a plate with some leftover sprouts.

It's not for me!

I place it outside the back door. For the knockers.

In Cornwall, Ted told me, you feed the knockers, the little faery folk, so they will help you.

I think Mum needs all the help she can get.

Nobody notices I've been out.

'I think I'll just pop upstairs a minute to see how your mum's getting on,' says Grandma as I slip back beside her.

'That's not fair!' protests V.

But then, from upstairs, comes a noise.

A high, squeaky noise.

Jellico sits bolt upright, ears pricked, and whines.

The noise comes again. Louder this time. Insistent.

Jellico stands up and barks, wagging his tail.

It sounds like a cat mewling.

Or a lamb bleating.

Or a...

'Baby!' beams Anika and we all run upstairs.

Mum is sitting up in bed holding a baby in her arms.

'Come and meet your new brother,' she smiles.

'Ted said it would be a boy!' I gasp.

'Ted was right,' says Mum.

'The best Christmas present in the world,' says Uncle Vez.

My baby brother has been born on Christmas night!

'Good timing!' says Dontie.

'We should call him Jesus!' suggests Stanley.

'I don't think you're allowed to,' says

Mum, who is looking very pink and pretty. 'Any more ideas?'

He's smooth and soft and damp. Like a little seal.

'Silkie,' I whisper, stroking his velvety cheek, and his tiny mouth twitches in approval.

Everyone laughs.

'Archibald,' declares Uncle Vez. 'Because he's bald like me.'

Everyone groans.

'Petroc,' says V.

'I'm not naming him after a pebble!' splutters Mum.

'Pablo,' suggests Dad. 'As in Pablo Picasso.'

'David,' says Grandma. 'After my father.'

'Benjamin,' says Granddad. 'After mine.'

'Zebadee,' says Dontie.

'Stanley,' says Anika.

We all gaze at the baby thoughtfully. None of them seems right. The baby doesn't look like an Archibald or a Petroc or a Pablo or a David or a Benjamin or a Zebadee, we've already got a Stanley and we can't call him Jesus.

'Will,' I say. 'His name is Will.'

Everything goes quiet.

'Will,' repeats Mum.

'Will,' says Dad, trying it out.

'Will,' says Uncle Vez. 'Good, strong name.'

'Will,' says Grandma. 'Very nice.'

'Will,' says Granddad. 'I like it.'

'Will's all right,' shrugs Dontie.

'Will's OK,' says V.

'Will.' Stanika beam at each other.

'Right then,' says Mum. 'Will it is. Good idea, Mattie.'

This has been the best Christmas ever.

Later that night, when everyone else is fast asleep, I open my bedroom window and peer outside.

There's a full moon and the sky is sprinkled with stars. It's a magical night.

Down on the doorstep, the turkey and sprouts have vanished from the plate.

The knockers have been and collected their fee for looking after the Butterfields.

I watch the sculptures in the garden standing like ghosts in the moonlight. Soon there will be another one joining them.

A silkie.

A seal.

For Will.

THE END

my Funny Family

CHRIS HIGGINS

my Funny Family

Illustrated by
Lee Wildish

Mattie is nine years old and she worries about everything, which isn't surprising. Because when you have a family as big and crazy as hers, there's always something to worry about! Will the seeds she's planted in the garden with her brothers and sisters grow into fruit and veg like everyone promised? Why does it seem as if Grandma doesn't like them sometimes? And what's wrong with Mum?

Read the first book in the hilarious and heart-warming young series about the chaotic life of the Butterfield family.

www.chrishigginsthatsme.com

Hodder Children's Books

my **Funny Family**

It's the summer holiday and the Butterfield family is going away to Cornwall. As usual, Mattie has plenty to worry about. What if she loses the luggage she's been put in charge of? What if someone falls over a cliff? And worst of all ... what if they've forgotten someone?

Read the second book in the hilarious and heart-warming *My Funny Family* series.

Also available as an ebook

www.chrishigginsthatsme.com

Hodder Children's Books

Before writing her first novel, Chris Higgins taught English and Drama for many years in secondary schools and also worked at the Minack, the open-air theatre on the cliffs near Lands End. She now writes full time and is the author of ten books for children and teenagers.

Chris is married with four daughters. She loves to travel and has lived and worked in Australia as well as hitchhiking to Istanbul and across the Serengeti Plain. Born and brought up in South Wales, she now lives in the far west of Cornwall with her husband.